THE CAR RACE

BY RACHEL BACH

AMICUS READERS 1 AMICUS INK

amicus readers

Say Hello to Amicus Readers.

You'll find our helpful dog, Amicus, chasing a ball—to let you know the reading level of a book.

1

Learn to Read

High frequency words and close photo-text matches introduce familiar topics and provide ample support for brand new readers.

2

Read Independently

Some repetition is mixed with varied sentence structures and a select amount of new vocabulary words are introduced with text and photo support.

3

Read to Know More

Interesting facts and engaging art and photos give fluent readers fun books both for reading practice and to learn about new topics.

Amicus Readers and Amicus Ink are imprints of Amicus
P.O. Box 1329, Mankato, MN 56002
www.amicuspublishing.us

Library of Congress Cataloging-in-Publication Data
Names: Bach, Rachel, author.
Title: The car race / by Rachel Bach.
Description: Mankato, Minnesota : Amicus, [2017] | Series: Let's Race
Identifiers: LCCN 2015041502 (print) | LCCN 2015047873 (ebook) | ISBN 9781607539124 (library binding) | ISBN 9781681510361 (eBook) | ISBN 9781681521312 (paperback)
Subjects: LCSH: Stock car racing--Juvenile literature. | NASCAR (Association)--Juvenile literature.
Classification: LCC GV1029.9.S74 B34 2017 (print) | LCC GV1029.9.S74 (ebook) | DDC 796.72--dc23
LC record available at http://lccn.loc.gov/2015041502

Editor: Wendy Dieker
Designer: Tracy Myers
Photo Researchers: Derek Brown and Aubrey Harper

Photo Credits: Daniel Huerlimann-BEELDE / Shutterstock.com cover, 3, 8-9, 16; Action Sports Photography / Shutterstock.com 5, 10-11, 14; ZUMA Press, Inc. / Alamy Stock Photo 6-7; Splash News / Corbis 13

Printed in the United States of America.

HC 10 9 8 7 6 5 4 3 2 1
PB 10 9 8 7 6 5 4 3 2 1

Let's watch the car race!

The drivers get ready.

REALTREE
TaxSlayer.com
NASCAR
RACE CAR
xfinity
SERIES
MSD
Coors LIGHT
POLE

CAT
IMPALA
PENNZOIL
CHARGER
500
WHELEN

The green flag starts the race. Zoom!

The cars race
for many laps.
The red car
is in the lead.
Who will win?

88
TaxSlayer
.com
Great Clips
Goody's
AMERICA'S POWER .ORG
Nationwide
Holley
3M
Edelbrock
SIMPSON
Auto Meter
JEGS
MSD
ARP

CAMRY

It is time
for a pit stop.
The crew puts
on new tires.

The race keeps going.

Oh no! A crash!

These cars are out.

DISCOUNT TIRE
32
CAMARO

INTERSTATE
MONSTER ENERGY
GOODYEAR
INTERSTATE BATTERIES
Outrageously Dependable

Who won?
Tina in the white car!
She gets the
checkered flag!

PARTS OF A RACE CAR